Stormdamage

BRIAN PATTEN

UNWIN
PAPERBACKS

LONDON SYDNEY WELLINGTON

First published in Great Britain by Unwin ® Paperbacks, an imprint of
Unwin Hyman Limited, in 1988.

Unwin Hyman Limited
15–17 Broadwick Street, London W1V 1FP

Allen & Unwin Australia Pty Ltd
8 Napier Street, North Sydney, NSW 2060, Australia

Allen & Unwin New Zealand Pty Ltd with the Port Nicholson Press
60 Cambridge Terrace, Wellington, New Zealand

British Library Cataloguing in Publication Data

Patten, Brian, *1946–*
Storm damage.
I. Title
821′.914[F]
ISBN 0-04-440146-9 Pbk

Set in 12/14 point Bodoni by
Rowland Phototypesetting Limited, Bury St Edmund, Suffolk
and printed in Great Britain by
The Bath Press, Avon

Acknowledgements

Three of these poems, 'The Apple Flavoured Worm', 'The Bee's Last Journey to the Rose' and 'The Complaint', first appeared in a book of verse for children. 'Job Hunting' was first published in *The Sunday Times*, and 'No' in *New Departures*. 'A Fallible Lecture' was suggested by Adrian Mitchell's poem, 'The Oxford Hysteria Of English Poetry'.

Contents

Storm damage

RIPE FOR CONVERSION

THE GOD-FREAKS, their bibles
Burning with improbable flames,
Have singled me out again.
Perhaps they see in me a pit
Only God can fill. Their thrill
Is to catch me on street corners
Or coming out of bars where their quarry,
The proletariat, gather.
Like salesmen whose patter devalues
The goods they are selling, they
Reduce Heaven and its prophets
To a crutch and a cliché.
They're like morose cenobites
Whose isolation is secular and spreads
From room to room, and is malignant.
Watching them forage so earnestly
Among the crowd they cannot encompass,
Sometimes out of charity I let
Their soul-squad catch me,
Listen to them talk until
They spill out their own history.
Yet it makes me uneasy the way
They see in me someone
Not so different from themselves;
A man exiled from himself,
In a state of mild decay, like a house
No one lives in any more,
Ripe for conversion.

THE AMBUSH

WHEN THE face you swore never to forget
Can no longer be remembered,
When a list of regrets are torn up and thrown away
Then the hurt fades,
And you think you've grown strong.
You sit in bars and boast to yourself,
'Never again will I be vulnerable.
It was an aberration to be so open,
A folly, never to be repeated.'
How absurd and fragile such promises.
Hidden from you, crouched
Among the longings you have suppressed
And the desires you imagine tamed,
A sweet pain waits in ambush.
And there will come a day when in a field
Heaven's mouth gapes open,
And on a web the shadow
Of a marigold will smoulder.
Then without warning,
Without a shred of comfort,
Emotions you thought had been put aside
Will flare up within you and bleed you of reason.
The routines which comforted you,
And the habits in which you sought refuge
Will bend like sunlight under water,
And go astray.

Your body will become a banquet,
Falling heavenwards.
You will loll in spring's sweet avalanche
Without the burden of memory,
And once again
Monstrous love will swallow you.

THE SHADOW-PUPPET'S COMPLAINT

NOT QUITE drunk yet, I lean across the table
And gossip with my shadow.
We have intimate conversations
About the day's non-events,
About where they are leading and
The brightness they have fled from.
It smiles at my attempts to give substance
To that skeleton, Memory.

My shadow munches on the shadow of an apple,
And does not fill me.

I listen in horror as it complains
Of the raw edge gone from love,
And though I wish to fault all it says
My arguments are insubstantial.
It has an army of confederates to back
Every claim it can make against me.

Like a shabby magician
It conjures up the past,
Parades before me
All my mistakes,
My indiscretions.
It has drawn into itself
Everything for which I hungered.

Even in darkness I cannot escape it:
At night I dream of a stream that flows
Undauntingly through all things,
That clears away longings so old
They have festered.
My shadow sits beside it, thirsting.

Recently an avalanche of deaths
Has softened its tongue.
It asks questions of me
So simple they can hardly be answered.
When did you last weep?
Was there a witness?

It has begun to speak of what is still felt
For a friend not seen these last few years.
It can no longer remember which of us
Loved her best,
Nor even if that love was real,
Or a shadow.

I remember once how after she had gone
I sat like this in a different room.
I think it was only my shadow that wept,
And went out into the night in search of her.

DRESS SENSELESS

AH, THE futility of it!
Spending so much time in front of mirrors
When the soul itself is threadbare.

AMOUR

SHE SAID I was a wolf in sheep's clothing.
Not true.
I was a lamb, in armour.

THE CONFESSION

WHEN HE showed her the photograph again, she
said,

'Yes, I remember taking it.
I was incredibly young then.
You handed me the camera
And telling me over and over how to use it
You posed, smiling stiffly.
You were so pompous, so blind to everything.

'It was a July afternoon.
The day was hot and my body hummed.
I was bored, and in search of an adventure
That seemed beyond you.

'Yet how can I forget that day?
Look closer at the photograph.
See there in the background,
In the corner behind you,
That other boy, grinning so openly.'

THE PACKAGE

AT DINNER, long-faced and miserable,
They cast sly glances at the other guests,
The pink-kneed husband and his wife
Sitting with their five-year old, complaining pest.
The holiday brochure they'd believed in, lied,
Still they blamed each other for the clouds
And ever since arriving they had rowed.

After dinner, the child put to bed,
They bickered beneath the hotel's vine
And the ghosts of false what-might-have-beens
Surfaced with each extra glass of wine.
Theirs was a package holiday all right:
    A package stuffed
With years of rootless longings and regrets.
Their bickering done, they sat mutely and both grieved
For what neither might have anyway achieved.

The next day they'd gone. They'd cut
Their holiday short, and carried back with them
A failure of another sort.
It was a failure to understand how all
Their arguments revolved around
An earlier package that they'd bought –
One promoted by both Church and State, one written
In the same tempting style; one over which
A watery sun had shone the same short while.

A Pity this Couldn't have been a Love Poem

PLEASE, DON'T talk so much!
Like little thieves
Your words steal affection,
Bury communication.
Don't talk so much of names that run
Like headless chickens through the daily press
And leave me unimpressed, or less.
Don't talk so much so early on,
Don't crowd the morning out with words
So that the hours sag
And rattle with a dry vocabulary
Of *I* and *I* and *I* and *me*.
How can a single tongue
Unearth so much trash?
It's like a stage on which
A multitude of egos prance.
I can't get close,
I can't get through
All the chatter and the prattle to
The core of you.

Once I'd have loved to sever
That verbal umbilical cord,
But now I am too tired,
Word-blasted, bored.

THE TRAGEDY

BEHIND THE cooker yesterday
I found a pencil-written note.
It had been there some years,
Brooding and awaiting its moment
Among the chip-fat and ketchup.

'Bastard,' it read,
'I'll not be back again.
It's after midnight. This time
I'm going forever.'

It was from someone whose name
I could not decipher.
Grease had obscured the signature.

I was not even sure whether
It was addressed to me.
Perhaps. Perhaps not.
I neither knew nor cared.

That is the tragedy.

DEAD THICK

No. I haven't kept up with the modern stuff.
Haven't read a book in years.
Textbooks? A few, but nothing new.
Mind you, it's not that I don't
Have the inclination, just that
Nothing's grabbed my fancy.

Still, I like what I've read: Hardy,
Golding, I'll flick through
Graham Greene if I have to.
But no, nothing new. Mind you
I read the reviews. They contain
A lot of sharp observation.
After reading a couple I find
I can form my own opinion.

I'm too busy for literature, that's the problem.
I'm after promotion. Ideally what I'd like
Is a job in administration.
What do I do? Teach. English.
It's exhausting. The kids are thick.
They've nothing between their ears.
Do you know what? Some of them
Haven't read a book in years.

GLUE STORY

JIMMY SMITH had a problem,
It's daft but it's true,
After so much glue-sniffing he imagined
Everything else he sniffed
Stuck to him too.

When he left school
The smell of dole-queues
Lit a fuse in his brain,
And though he tried to keep his nose clean
The smell of failure
Would not go away.

The smell of money
Obsessed him by its absence,
And there was no evading
How the smell of Borstal
Was all pervading.

It was either being sentenced
To the dole-queue or the army,
So having little to lose
And even less to gain
One day when pissed
Jimmy decided to enlist.

He was trained in less time than it takes
To train an alsatian dog.
He became completely dependable
And utterly expendable,
And was packed off to Ulster
Like a parcel no one wanted.

The estates were similar to his own,
The walkways stank,
Smelt the same.
At first Belfast seemed
A daft kid's game.

But soon enough paranoia
Blossomed on street corners.
The smell of blood stuck to him,
And the smell of politicians' lies
Hovered round his nose like flies.

And when he shot a child
His excuses were thin,
And the smell of rubber bullets
Haunted him.

It's daft, but it's true:
When Jimmy blew his own brains out
No one blamed the system,
They blamed the glue.

THE LOST PASSPORT

'Sadly once again I cannot visit.
My application for a passport has been refused.'

— from a letter

HALINA HAS lost her passport.
She is standing in a street in Warsaw
Fumbling in her handbag.

'I had it a moment ago,' she says,
'A moment ago!'

Halina stops people in the street.
She asks them to help her
Look for the lost passport.

Poor Halina.
Hush, my dear,
Your talk is crazy.

Perhaps she lost it in Lwôw.
Perhaps her passport
Is asleep under the snow.

Perhaps a little Russian squirrel
Has stolen Halina's passport.

Anyway, it is lost.
Under the Polish earth its date,
1939, is frozen.

Halina stands at the tram-stop,
Drunk on vodka and memory;
She asks the flower-sellers,

'Have you seen it?
I had it a moment ago.
A moment ago.'

WHERE ARE ALL THOSE LONG-HAIRED OPTIMISTS NOW?

WHERE ARE all those long-haired optimists now?
The barbers are standing over their graves, gloating.

In attics and basements
Their children are playing
With junk-beads,

Inside the yellow, infantile magazines
That celebrated ghost-revolutions
Earwigs are nesting,

In crematoriums
Old protest songs are regurgitated
As piped muzak.

So much hoped for, so little altered:

On the stock market
Community workshops
Appear as listed companies.

Outside
The same truncheons
Rising and falling,

Batons conducting
Man's history, ignoring
His passing fashions, his illusions.

PERHAPS

AND WHEN you turn your back something
That will not happen again happens,
And when you close your eyes perhaps
The stars rush about,
Or something changes colour.

And if you had been in a certain cafe,
In a certain street at a certain time,
Perhaps she would not have risen
And putting on a blue coat, vanished.

You hurry, and every place you pass
Pass places you have never been,
Where the future comes and goes,
Swirls round you and bypasses.

And all your dithering days you go
About the business of living,
Only for you it is not exactly living,
But filing away, ticking off, rearranging.

And nothing will ever be repeated again
Exactly as it happened,
And so much will have been missed
That has never been missed,
And yet still leaves you hungry and baffled.

THE BEE'S LAST JOURNEY TO THE ROSE

I CAME FIRST through the warm grass
Humming with Spring,
And now swim through the evening's
Soft sunlight gone cold.
I'm old in this green ocean,
Going a final time to the rose.

North wind, until I reach it
Keep your icy breath away
That changes pollen into dust.
Let me be drunk on this scent a final time,
Then blow if you must.

UNDETERRED

I PUT MY hand into the lucky dip.
It was full of acid.
Undeterred, believing luck
Something with which
One has to grapple,
I dipped my hand
Into a barrel of worms,
Pulled out an apple.

THE CYNIC'S ONLY LOVE POEM

LOVE COMES and goes
And often it has paused,
Then comes back to see
The damage it has caused.

THE APPLE-FLAVOURED WORM

WHEN THE rivers were pregnant with fishes
And the trees were pregnant with buds,
When the earth was fat with seeds
And a million other goods,
Taking a snooze in an apple
Was an apple-flavoured worm.
It heard God's voice say, 'Bite.
Eve, it is your turn.'

When the sky was bluer than blue
And the earth shone bright as a pin,
Before Paradise has been abandoned
Or a tongue had invented a sin,
Taking a snooze in an apple
Was the apple-flavoured worm.
It heard God's voice say, 'Bite.
Adam, it's now your turn.'

Then the bloom was gone from the garden,
The first petal had dropped from a flower,
The wound in the rib's cage was healed
And Satan had lived for an hour.
And wide awake in the apple
The apple-flavoured worm
Heard the Gates of Heaven closing
And a key of iron turn.

THE WHALE'S HYMN

ON AN ocean before cold dawn broke
Covered by an overcoat
I lay awake in a tiny boat
And heard a whale.

Hearing a song so solemn and so calm
It seemed absurd to feel alarm –
For I had a notion it sang
God's favourite hymn,

And spoke direct to Him.

No

No. NO thank you, but no. No, not just yet, no.
Later perhaps, perhaps some other time.
Maybe in a few moments. Maybe tomorrow, only no
Not now, no. I might but, but no I couldn't,
No I can't, the problem is I'm not allowed. No,
I'm unable to. It's impossible. No, it's –
What? Yes, I know, but no.

When you think of the things you have lost
And wish to find again,
When you've summoned up the courage needed
To rid yourself of the junk accumulated,
You can be sure No will make its appearance.
When you wonder why there are things the tongue
Can no longer haul up from the soul,
You'll find it's No that weighs them down.

For No holds sway in the hierarchy of words.
With its retinue of doubts
It comes sneaking through the blood.
It infests your resolutions,
Sabotages your ambitions.
It squats inside you like a goblin,
Distributing poisons.
It has a fat bagful of reasons,
An excuse for everything.

How lovely it would be to be cured of No!
Eh? What? Me? I can? Take the cure? Now?

No. No thank you, but no. No, not just yet no.
Later perhaps, perhaps some other time.
Maybe in a few mo

YES

LAST NIGHT I dreamt again of Adam returning
To the Garden's scented, bubbling cauldron.

Eve was beside him,
Their shadows were cut adrift
And the hum of bees was in their blood,

And the world was slow and good and all
The warm and yawning newness of their flesh
Was fixed forever in the glow of 'Yes'.

POISONING DOWN

IT'S MOSTLY the old who fall victim to the rain.
When senility sets in they forget
How much the world has changed.
Though you try to stop them,
Though you try to warn them over and over again,
Still the poor old sods
Go hobbling out into the rain.

Sometimes in front of children
You have to shut them up –
Their influence is worse than bad:
'Mummy! Mummy, did you hear what Granny said?
She said she used to go out walking in the rain!
Look, she's trying now. She's fiddling with the door
    again,
And its absolutely poisoning down!'

You can tell the kids Granny's mad –
That she's gaga and all old folk
Are living in a fantasy,
But sooner or later they are bound to see
Old movies that confirm the truth.
(Thank God there is an outcry to demand
Films like *Singing in the Rain* are banned.)

The trouble is,
You can't ban the old from remembering the past
Or from wanting to relive
Sensations that seem abnormal now.
All you can really do is tell the kids,
'Don't believe a word poor Granny's said.'

Soon enough her generation will be gone,
And all those who ever walked out in the rain
Will be an archaic memory, and dead.

Festival Vampires

THEY TRAVEL up through the night
  in first-class coffins,
The young would-be producers,
  the media-vampires;
Signing in at the best hotels they scan
  the fringe programme for what
Can be watered down; packaged.
  These superior, talentless beings
Will make no mistakes –
  gay Othellos and lesbian Macbeths
Do not fit easily
  between commercial breaks.

The young playwrights whose typewriters
  have rattled a year with discord,
The comedians who refuse to abandon jokes
  about limp pricks, monogrammed vibrators,
The maniacs whose talent, uncategorised,
  burns and strolls across ice –
These and others lost within their passions
  are dismissed as pointless.

In wine bars and in the best restaurants
    the media-vampires talk Beckett
And think ratings.
    It's a media cattle-market,
Not a festival they're attending.
    They charm the names
And ignore the nameless,
    They smile and are discreet
And all the while their eyes are peeled
    For a jaunty, updated
Coronation Street.

ORACLE

WHO WOULD have guessed the owner
Of the Greek fish and chip shop
Was such a prophet?
The owner of the Greek fish and chip shop
Is truly an Oracle.

Caught up in the riot, staggering
Through the smoke and flames
I saw on the chip shop window
An ominous message:
'FRYING TONIGHT!'

CREATURE COMFORTS

My CREATURE comforts no longer comfort me.
Truth is, they never did.
It was always the thought
Of leaving them behind
Was the luxury.

CAT-NAP

When YOU gathered together
The clothes drunkenness scattered
The cat came, sniffing at ghosts,
Prowling the bed in search
Of what should have been there.
Puzzled by your scent still on me
And by your absence
It nestled down where you might have stayed,
Would have stayed had not
Guilt sent you crying, flying
Homewards, husbandward
From your small, snatched triumph.

AS SHE GOES HOME
THIS EVENING

As SHE goes home this evening,
As she goes home
Her head and body still full of him,
What can she say
To the one who waits impatient,
Who waits in a room rehearsing
A list of stale arguments,
Adding up and subtracting,
Like a sickly accountant,
A registry of hurts?
What reasons can be given,
What excuses can be made
So late in the evening,
As she goes home
Her head and body singing,
Singing and knowing
No reasons are needed?
For all her excuses are vanishing
And all her guilts are melting,
And she is careless finally
And is finally loving,
And is wearing the scent of the one
From whom she is walking
As evidence for the one
To whom she is going
For a final time
So late in the evening.

WOUND-CREAM

PERHAPS IT is the way Love's promoted;
You'd think it came in a jar,
Something that could be spread
Over all that bothers us –
A heal-all, a wound-cream,
A media promoted fairy-tale
Gutted of darkness.

Though its contradictions
Nail us to each other
And the hunger for it
Can be our undoing,
We still use it as a prop,
As proof we are living.

How hard to do other than
Give it precedence, forgetting
How friendship outlives it,
Commits fewer crimes,
Wears its name at times.

Autumn Joke

I THOUGHT IT was her hurrying behind me,
About to say, 'Stop, nothing's changed!'
But it was only an old sycamore leaf
Blown by the wind, the joker.

Nothing but the Truth

POLICING ONESELF is difficult.
The evidence that has been mounting up:
White-washed, all of it.

Dear Maurice

Seventy. TIME to escape committees.
It's the perfect excuse to go awol,
Play the recluse, cock-a-snook
At all that's stupid and obtuse.
Seventy. Never in a muddle.
You're fit as a bell and
Sound as a fiddle.
Free now to be a goliard,
To look inward (or drink,
Get plastered; experiment
With banana custard).

Please put up a while longer
With the body's tricks.
Though aches and pains may roam
Like bullies through the veins,
Hooligans at large, fight off
Their attempts at sabotage.
What's one kidney more
(or less).

Better instead to bugger off
To France or Tituana, leave
The kids to puzzle out Nirvana.

Even if it's only for our sakes
Hang around a bit.
Get fit. Take up hang-gliding
Or sports still more sublime
(i.e. run circles round
Wittgenstein). You're not ready yet
To jog Heavenward.

Old Ladies in the Church-yard

At last I understand religion's sway
Over the poor crowd,
The frightened counting bead by bead
All their lonely follies;
Frail ladies wandering at light's edge
Believing in a place where Spring
And its mass of blossom waits
Behind a gate pain cannot enter.
It's not called Paradise by them, but Heaven –
God's vast dose of valium that makes
          their terror possible.

And all their fuzzy notions of that place
Rise, lark-pure, above my reasoning,
And sometimes I want to join them there
In that special atmosphere
Where sense is made of all despair.

At the grave's edge this evening the snowdrops
– Those little ballerinas shivering in the grey soil –
Have forgotten what dying was and are back again,
Without memory of frost,
With no notion of pain.

I bend to touch them. The carcass creaks,
A rook's nest of bone and tissue in which
The soul sways, and is blown by doubt.
And unlike those frail ladies
Can work nothing out.

A Prayer Seeking God's Protection from Over-enthusiastic Young Priests

LORD, FORGIVE me half my sins
And I will forgive all yours
If only you'd stop young priests
From playing bass-guitars
Or attending fancy dress dos
Dressed up to the hilt
In togas and nice dresses
That confirm their guilt.
Dear Lord, I only half-believe
And as the years pass
I do get rather curious
About the meaning of the mass,

So let me meet a priest of substance
To whom the serious have confessed
But don't land me in the vestry
With a priestly little pest.
I would like to be more spiritual
As grief and the years unroll
But I simply can't abide young priests
Who play mindless rock and roll.
They've got their act together,
Their message, so glib and pat,
Shines in day-glow on the notice board:
'GOD IS WHERE IT'S AT!'
(Sometimes in their company
I think I smell a rat.)
The Church is wise and meaningful
But O my dear Lord
Do send a little brimstone
To clean up the notice-board.

I know I am reactionary
And that Christ Himself was young,
But he did not wear designer jeans
When He addressed the throng.
I do so much want to believe
It almost is a joke
When the priest is young and smart-arsed
And stoned on wine and coke.
I might accept the dogma,
Get to understand the creed,
But I'm fucked if I'm confessing to
A priest looking like Lou Reed.

JOB HUNTING

ON THE wasteland that stretches
From here to the river
My children play a game.
It is called job hunting.
They blacken their faces,
And with knives and imitation guns
They go stalking among
The lichen-coated ruins
Of broken machinery and cranes.
It is an exciting game.
Sometimes they come back exhausted,
Clutching objects they have prised
From the earth –
Nuts, bolts, the broken vizor
Of a welder's mask.
'Daddy,' they ask, 'Daddy,
Is this a job? Can we keep it?'

THE SANE SOLUTION
A cautionary tale

AFTER THE revolution, when the dead
Were banished to graveyards
And certain place-names changed
The new dictator declared, 'It is time
For massive changes. Our armies
Are tired fighting. Our poets
Are tired protesting. Even our cooks
Are jaded and are lamenting
The poverty of their ingredients.'

Locked in his palace the insane one
Sought a sane solution.
It came, he said, in a vision brought
By an angel that shook with laughter.
'Poets must be shown how to assemble weapons.
Cooks must take up the pen
In defence of free-speech.
Soldiers must become cooks.'

His message spread across incredulous borders.
In embassies the world over ambassadors
Grinned, discussed how long before
El Loco's downfall. But to dismiss the insane
Is itself insanity. Years later,
And still he sits there
Dictating volumes of twisted wisdom.
And no country is quite so peaceful.
And no country is quite so docile.

When visited by the baffled
Representatives of foreign powers
He does not hesitate to point out
The simplicity of his solution.
'Who cares,' he asks,
'If poets aim guns at clouds?
Who listens to the outraged cries of bad cooks?
Tell me señor, when was the last time
A rebel soldier pulled the pin from a chicken
And tossed it over the palace walls?'

20 Million Flies

5 MILLION FLIES 5 million flies
Can you tell me where they're going
5 million flies?

Another 5 million flies another 5 million flies
They must be going somewhere
10 million flies

10 million flies 10 million flies
Can you tell me where they're going
10 million flies?

10 million flies 10 million flies
And here come another
10 million flies

20 million flies 20 million flies
And buzzing through the mildewed air
Another 20 million flies

40 million flies 40 million flies
They must be going somewhere
40 million flies

They're going to lay their eggs
In nose and mouth and eyes
And soon each will have its own corpse

80 million flies? 80 million flies?
A corpse for each and every one
Of 80 million flies?

Dancing in England

Dancing is a political act
                    quote from a TV documentary

THE DANCERS kept on dancing
And did not hear the shout
From the corner of the ballroom
Where the lights were going out.

Northern Subjects

SUCH A weight of power sits on her shoulders?
Then how come she's not hunched up
like her northern subjects?
It's the weight of privilege, I suppose,
lightens the burden.

Hair Today, No Her Tomorrow

'I'VE BEEN upstairs,' she said.
'Oh yes?' I said.
'I found a hair,' she said.
'A hair?' I said.
'In the bed,' she said.
'From a head?' I said.
'It's not mine,' she said.
'Was it black?' I said.
'It was,' she said.
'I'll explain,' I said.
'You swine,' she said.
'Not quite,' I said.
'I'm going,' she said.
'Please don't,' I said.
'I hate you!' she said.
'You do?' I said.
'Of course,' she said.
'But why?' I said.
'That black hair,' she said.
'A pity,' I said.

'Time for truth,' she said.
'For confessions?' I said.
'Me too,' she said.
'You what?' I said.
'Someone else,' she said.
'Oh dear,' I said.
'So there!' she said.

'Ah well,' I said.
'Guess who?' she said.
'Don't say,' I said.
'I will,' she said.
'You would,' I said.
'Your friend,' she said.
'Oh damn,' I said.
'And his friend,' she said.
'Him too?' I said.
'And the rest,' she said.
'Good God,' I said.

'What's that?' she said.
'What's what?' I said.
'That noise?' she said.
'Upstairs?' I said.
'Yes,' she said.
'The new cat,' I said.
'A cat?' she said.
'It's black,' I said.
'Black?' she said.
'Long-haired,' I said.
'Oh no,' she said.
'Oh yes,' I said.
'Oh shit!' she said.
'Goodbye,' I said.

'I lied,' she said.
'You lied?' I said.
'Of course,' she said.

'About my friend?' I said.
'Y-ess,' she said.
'And the others?' I said.
'Ugh,' she said.
'How odd,' I said.
'I'm forgiven?' she said.
'Of course,' I said.
'I'll stay?' she said.
'Please don't,' I said.
'But why?' she said.
'I lied,' I said.
'About what?' she said.
'The new cat,' I said.
'It's white,' I said.

SNIPPETS

INFIDELITIES?
Snippets of truth scissored
From giant lies.

TWO BIRDS FROM NOWHERE
Or, the etymologist's lament

OUT OF *nowhere* he rescued *heron*.
While dawn peeled away a river's darkness
He sent it flying towards her;

And out of that same word he rescued *wren*.
It slipped through the wounds of its tormentors
Into a fortress of bramble.

These creatures were a gift to her,
Brought out of the nowhere in which
He found himself,

A tongue-tied etymologist
Horrified by his ability
To rescue *nothing* from *love*.

THE WRONG HOUSE

I WENT INTO a house full of people writing notes.
'Hush,' they said, 'move quietly here, don't dance or shout;
We are the poets exploring this and that,
Examining daylight, odds and ends of a universe.'

I thought, obviously this is the wrong house.
This is the house I've spent my life avoiding.
It was you I meant to visit – you poetry,
Who has always spring in the brain, whose house
Is unquestioningly brilliant.

'Sit down,' they said. 'Your first lesson's this:
Make sure for each line you write
You write another that can explain it.
Keep these, along with useful addresses,
In a separate notebook.

'And now here is a pen and here
Is a scribbling pad. For inspiration
Some object of immense beauty will soon
Be brought before you. Study carefully.
Let your examination be detached. Professional.'

On a plate they brought a dead nightingale,
The remnants of its song
Dribbled down the willow-pattern.
'Dip your pen in this,' they said, 'the results
Are satisfying, the sonnets stupendous.'

APHASIA

Aphasia is a condition which affects the comprehension and initiation of speech, and causes great mental distress. The poem was written for the Association of All Speech Impaired Children (AFASIC)

I'M SEVEN, and I'm dead bright,
But words give me a fright.
Words are bullies.
Sneaky things. They gabble and lie.
Sometimes trying to understand
Them makes me cry. Words hurt.
Words are all over the place.
They get shoved in my face.
I don't know why but
Words make me cry.

I wish words were things
You could hug,
Or that they smelt nice.
I wish they came in bottles
Like fizzy-drinks, or melted
Like ice-cream. But they don't.
Words are mean. They bully me.
Lock me away
From what I want to say.

I can't even ask for help,
And I'm only seven
(And a bit).
Words spread nasty gossip.
They must. Otherwise why
Would people think I'm thick?

Words,
They make me sick
Inside.

LOOKING BACK ON IT (AGAIN)

AT NINETEEN I was a brave old hunchback,
Climbing to tremendous heights,
Preparing to swing down on my golden rope
And rescue Accused Innocence.

But on my swooping, downward path one day
Innocence ducked,
And I amazed at such an act
Crashed into a wall she had been building.

Twenty-one years later,
Sitting stunned beside that same brick wall
I see others climbing their golden ropes
And hear Innocence sniggering.

I say nothing much,
But sit with bandages and the hope
That maybe after all
Some sweet fool might in time
Swing right through that wall.

BLOOD BROKER
Or, the Threadneedle Street vampire

IN MY office in the City
Is a coffin lined with shares.
At night I sleep there,
Bloated on an endless trickle of information.
Survivor of a dynasty that stretches back
 Deep into Transylvanian bank-vaults
I have a unique hunger.

Excommunicated from the world of the living
I stalk the stock-market floor,
A shadow among dealers, a whisper amongst computers.
The ebb and flow of oil does not concern me,
Public companies are the terrain of zombies.
Their souls, lobotomised by greed,
Cling like moths to the flickering index.
I have no wish to speculate in properties
The graveward wind will blow away.
Over and over again I have seen
How time consolidates
The merger of maggot and banker.

To my colleagues I am something of an enigma.
My obsession with statistics concerning
The production of plasma
Baffles them.

The ownership of all blood-banks
Is my soul ambition.
And with blood collectors complaining
About the growing lack of raw material
I lick my lips,
Praise AIDS and all things venereal.
For I have done my sums,
The rarer a thing is
The more valuable it becomes,
And the deep well of human blood is running dry.
It is time to buy.

For soon on the Blood Exchange
There will be a bonanza the likes of which
The market's not seen before.
With each new disease and disaster
Shares in my private wells of human blood will soar.
And if there is an outcry against me
From the poor who will never afford me
I will not care. Around my coffin will be placed
A cordon of gnomes and ministers to protect me.
For I will own the bank that bleeds.

Already outside the sweet mouth of hell
A line of financiers wait to consult me.

BARE NECESSITY

NOW THAT I am free
Of all that might be said
To keep and entrap me,
How much deeper the need
To keep her beside me.

When romance flakes away
And infatuation vanishes
How much more clearly I see her.
From beneath all I have
Superimposed upon her
The skeleton rises.

Love, how stark the light needed
To see through your disguises,
To see through to where
One can begin to find her.

THE SECOND DOVE

PLEASE SIR,
Weren't there two doves in the Ark?
Yes, two.

Then what happened to the second dove,
To the one left unpraised, uncelebrated?
Sitting up there in the Ark's creaking rafters
Did it fester with jealousy?

And the dove Noah chose,
Was it God suggested it?
Or was the choice arbitrary?

All his life such questions obsessed him.

Old now, he lies in a hospice,
His body, his own Ark,
Adrift in a sea of sweat,
Is creaky and dying,

And through all his pain there threads
A song that leads him from panic,
The song of the one not chosen, the one
Left behind to comfort him.

THE COMPLAINT

'IT WILL not last!'

'Who said that?' demanded the dragonfly,
Morning-blown, oblivious to sorrow.

'The best has passed!'

'Who blasphemed just then?'
Inquired the wren.

'All perishes!'

'How absurd,' said the gnat,
'What idiot believes that?'

All listened for an answer.
None came.

Night fell on Paradise,
Its children slept.
Hunched outside the Gates Adam wept.

Salvage Operation

THOSE PARTS of myself I let escape –
Where did they go?
Marauding bands of sentiment
That crossed the heart's
Hardening frontier.
Where did they end up,
Those qualities thrown aside
And now sought again,
So late on, and in such earnest?
All those strands of the self
That fled as the soul corroded,
They must have sought refuge, but where?
Believing they can be nowhere other
Than submerged inside me
Almost nightly now I search for them,
But trawling through physical paranoia
Find little but fragments to remind me
Of the brightness wasted.
Yes because beginning over again
Is a fairy-tale the grave denies us,
And because there is still
Much gathering in to be done,
Many repatriations to be attempted,
Dive again, dreamer,
Back down into the currents of the mutable self
Where all that was lost might still drift,
Battered, but salvageable.

GOING TO DINNER

GOING TO dinner after many years away
I met a group of friends again today.
It should have come as no surprise to find them
    changed –
The girls were women now,
And though they looked as beautiful to me
Meeting in a claustrophobic, overtidy house,
It still came as a shock to see
Imposed over all that loveliness
Another face,
One that robbed of earlier radiance seemed to say,
'I made a choice, and was strong-willed enough
To put a dream or two aside. Yet I did not expect
To submerge identity in this
Routine of mind-numbing ordinariness.'

    And the men?
Everything had seemed within their reach.
High-fliers all! I had been envious
Of their wit, their charm, their confidence
That left me feeling so naive.
But now it seems they do not have so much to say.
Ambitions are modified,
And something in them once wide awake has died.

I felt sad and at a loss —
In no way justified to find
For some the world had shrunk
To a bleak suburban house.
And I could not help but think
How in time that house itself might shrink
From a mortgage to a mortician's bill.

Awkward there, on edge.
As if at some dreadful interview,
I wondered what in turn they made of me.

Single still; turning up alone in places where
Couples seemed the norm
I wondered if they thought I'd failed somewhere,
Being, as I've always been,
The kind of man who finds it hard to share
Someone else's domestic mess and small
Or grandiose and self-induced despair.

Going to dinner after many years away
Other faces showed more easily than mirrors can
How time blitzkriegs the average man.

    Anchored to routines,
Needing to believe my years away
Were wasted years, with good grace
These lovely people invited me back
Into the numbing fold.

I left. Upstairs a baby slept.
Beside the fence a child's bike was locked,
And passing through the gate, that cycle mocked
The tenuous freedom to which I'd clung
As years and friendships passed.

Yet perhaps I give that dinner too much weight.
Perhaps for them
The major drawback of the single man
Is that he buggers up the seating plan.

AT THE BACK OF THE A TO Z

SOMEWHERE AT the back of the A to Z
wondering,
What is it bolts these places to the earth?
They're so far from anything I know –
These flimsy fortresses in suburbs marooned
Behind the city's sodium-encrusted arteries,

Their anonymity guarding against doubts that,
Light as airborne seeds,
Bump bump bump against the double-glazing,
Then drift off again, finding, like myself,
No anchorage here.

THE WANT

WHERE DO longings go
When we let them go
And say we do not care?

They do not vanish into air,
But mingling with the blood
Create a poison there.

And where now the want,
The ache without a wound
That beat slow-time in the heart's
Once new-found core?

Relinquished,
Abandoned, all
That was raw?

BOTTLE-TALK

WHEN YOU have turned away
From the crowds and the bars
That first shaped then owned you
Don't convince yourself
It was they that harmed you.
Isolation disfigures men who think
Their separateness superior.
It was not fulfilling
The things you longed for
First shamed you;
Each day belittled
By the night's
Drunken exhaltations.
And each dawn the same
Comic-opera re-enacted:
Sober and cautious you watch
As all your resolutions fade
Back into dream-status.
Those intentions were merely bottle-talk,
Inconsistent ambitions
Dull days ignited.
There is only this certainty –
By the bottle's genie
None of your wishes
Will ever be granted.

Out To Lunch

'I HATE THIS bloody shop.
It's closed again.
Every time I come the bloody place is closed.
There's always this notice saying
"Out to lunch." As if I'm fooled.
You can't take two hours to eat.'

She's standing outside the antique shop in the cold,
An o.a.p. whose pension's stretched so far
It's about to snap as surely as her mind
Is about to snap.
She's brought along a lamp-stand made of wood.
Its shade's as yellow as her skin,
In its neck's a broken bulb that won't come out,
And like her veins its flex is grey and thin.

'I want to sell them this.
I've had it years –
It's old.'

She shakes the lamp. The plate-glass window shows
A bag-lady surfacing through Oxfam clothes.
And beyond the glass, in pools of light
The ornate chairs and tables mock
The junk to which she clings like straw.
'I was here yesterday, and the day before.
I won't come again. It's too bloody cold
And I'm not having them taking up my time.
Out to lunch? Two hours? It's a crime.'

THE ALMOST LOVELESS ALPHABET

NOT MANY streets away
                        A
is deciding to leave
                    B
who is sobbing and
                    C
is saying how
                D
has left
        E
for
    F
who is only half-listening to
                                G
complaining that
                    H
has left
        I
for
    J.

And lying in a ward somewhere,
wholly forgotten by
                        K
and
    L
and
    N

is
  O,
whose grief is terminal.

And
    P
has closed his ears to
                  Q
who is squabbling with
                        R
over what
          S
has done.

Meanwhile
          T
comforts
          U
who waits for
              V
to return.

And of course
              W
desires
      X
who does not know why
                      Y
desires
      Z,
who desires nothing.

And somewhere
(Thank god somewhere)
                     Mmmm
is sucking a delicious sweet
and is humming
a nice little tune.

HER FATHER RODE A HORSE CALLED DEATH

HER FATHER rode a horse called Death.
'Daddy, do not ride,' she said.
She prayed her father would not ride away.

It was a childish prayer, nothing new:
'Dear God, let me ride into death before
My mother or my father do.'

But God's ears were full of other prayers, or wax.
Her father galloped into death.
She held her breath:

Each hoof-print was deep and dark and hurt,
And each clod flung from the earth
Left a wound that bled.

And now between her father's death and her
Stands a pasture into which
The years have rolled and have obscured
The smaller details of her love,

And the hoofs of the horse on which he rode
Now echo through her own child's head.
'Mummy, do not go,' she said.

A FALIBLE LECTURE ON THE HISTORY OF ENG. LIT. FROM 1386 TO THE PRESENT

A FALIBLE LECTURE

Eng. Lit. was established one sunny
afternoon in 1386 when a gang of people
went for a walk to a place called Canterbury
They had a fantastic time swopping dirty
stories which someone called Chaucer wrote
down thereby establishing the fact that Eng.
Lit. is based on a collection of dirty jokes
After Chaucer Eng. Lit. dozed off until
Shakespeare began writing plays about
murder mayhem and paranoic Danish
princes In the course of one of his early plays
a woman is raped has her hands cut off and
her tongue cut out her father cuts his own
hand off two boys are hung up on meat hooks
their throats are slit and their flesh is served
up in a pie which their mother eats As you
can guess the audience of the day loved this
kind of stuff They went wild and
Shakespeare became famous. He predates
the video-nasty by over 400 years

Hanging around at the same time was Ben Jonson an apprentice brick-layer and murderer who devised a cunning method of escaping the gallows While in prison awaiting execution he discovered that by writing socially acceptable poetry hordes of literary-minded clerics would howl for his freedom The present day enthusiasm shown by hardened criminals for Open University courses in sociology and literature can be traced directly back to this fine playwright Next came John Donne who wrote some of the most sensual poems in the english language He became religious and then wrote some of the most sensual sermons in the english language He died in 1631 leaving poetry in the hands of John Milton who grew up and wrote Paradise Lost He survived King James Cromwell Fire Blindness Plague the death of his daughter and of two wives and then published Paradise Regained

In his wake trailed a bunch of young cynics
led by Dryden who invented literary
criticism in order that his verses could be
studied at places like Oxford These verses
bored some students so much they committed
suicide Unfortunately by then Dryden had
been dead for three hundred years and no
one could pin the blame on him Then along
came John Wilmot Earl of Rochester who
wrote satirical poems about dildos which
were entering fashionable British society in
the 1660s Also lurking about during this
period was a clergyman who wrote what is
possibly the most misogynistic poem in the
english language Called 'A Beautiful Young
Nymph Going To Bed' it is about a whore
with running sores who loses her false teeth
and whose glass eye is stolen by a rat His
name was Jonathan Swift and he also wrote
Gulliver's Travels which a few centuries
later was gutted and reduced to a fairy-tale
by real live lilliputians

This was the Age of Reason It was dominated by Alexander Pope and little of great beauty or passion was written because everybody was going about feeling incredibly reasonable After Pope came Samuel Johnson who compiled a dictionary and then everybody was going about feeling ashamed because they suddenly discovered they couldn't spell The first genius after this was William Blake who saw fairies in trees and who wrote erotic lines such as 'Bring me my arrows of desire' which utterly confused generations of school-children when it was turned into a hymn and sung in assemblies

Soon afterwards an opium-based drug called laudanum came on the market and all the poets became woozy and began writing romantic poetry One of these was John Keats who set a fashion for catching syphilis and TB and for dying young preferably in Italy Other poets followed his example Shelley even improving on it by drowning in Italy. Not wanting to be outdone Lord Byron committed incest with his half-sister went over to Italy to catch TB and drown but didn't and so instead he tried to unite the Greeks against the Turks. He was full of revolutionary fervour but unfortunately caught fever and died. He was very romantic The sole survivor of the romantic poets was William Wordsworth who decided to play it safe by living with his sister in the Lake District and writing poems about daffodils

Wordsworth felt paranoic every time his friend Coleridge came to visit him Coleridge was famous for standing outside churches bothering wedding guests by waving dead albatrosses in their faces He also invented marvellous excuses for not finishing his poems Though Wordsworth cornered the market in nature nothing he wrote had the authenticity of John Clare, a Norfolk peasant who was incarcerated in lunatic asylums for 28 years after a doctor decided he was insane through 'years addicted to poetic prosings' After his death it was rumoured that a group of doctors wanted to procure his corpse in order to open his brain and find out where the poetry came from Clare already knew where it came from: from clods of earth and from watching raindrops glittering on the backs of frogs.

Then the Victorians came and then they went
leaving behind an imperialistic farce about a
gang of bloodthirsty idiots who went
charging off in the wrong direction and got
clobbered, and a masterpiece about a Dong
with a luminous nose

The first of the great moderns was W. B. Yeats Critics like to stress how Yeats is one of the few poets whose poems were even more sensual in his old age than in his youth However most fail to point out that a series of monkey-gland operations carried out in a Swiss clinic by an austrian doctor obsessed with hormone therapy probably contributed considerably towards this Living in Yeats's shadow was the minor irish poet Alfred Noyes who rose briefly to fame when his poem 'All night he slept beneath the stars' was printed in the Irish Times as 'All night he slept beneath the stairs' He was praised for his realism

Next came D. H. Lawrence who was prosecuted posthumously for writing about the various uses to which aristocratic ladies could put daisy-chains He was followed by T. S. Eliot a rather dry american suffering under the delusion that he was an english bank manager While Eliot was writing a musical for Andrew Lloyd Webber Dylan Thomas was slaving away by lamplight composing some of the finest begging letters in the history of literature Until recently poetry was in the hands of a shy librarian from Hull who wrote about the kind of everyday things much admired by the english such as boredom, negation and death At the moment it resides with a yorkshireman who writes about belligerent natural forces and sheep

LOVE POEMS

HER SONG

For no other reason than I love him wholly
I am here; for this one night at least
The world has shrunk to a boyish breast
On which my head, brilliant and exhausted, rests,
And can know of nothing more complete.

Let the dawn assemble all its guilts, its worries
And small doubts that, but for love, would infect
This perfect heart.
I am as far beyond doubt as the sun.
I am as far beyond doubt as is possible.

GRAVE GOSSIP

Although Patten seeks to illuminate the commonplace,
the images used are fresh, bold and striking: the man
who gate-crashes Paradise, the mule that dreams of
becoming articulate, the drunken tightrope-walkers, the
moth with 'no memory of flames', the animate and
menacing telephone.

WAVES

And the one throwing the lifebelt,
Even he needs help at times,
Stranded on the beach,
Terrified of the waves.

NOTES TO THE HURRYING MAN

'A magic ability to turn radiant imagination loose in the
cities and streets and lonely bedrooms of modern living.'
The Times

LITTLE JOHNNY'S CONFESSION

'his poems . . . are newspaper captions that need no
photographs . . . loving creatures which survive all
newspapers.'
Adrian Mitchell

VANISHING TRICK

'a truthful and tender sequence of love poems, or poems
of the death of love; but it is also about the drive into
oneself ... the shedding of false images of oneself created
by other people. The poems write in a very assured way
about being diffident and vulnerable'
D.M. Thomas

'Patten is taking on the intricacies of love and beauty
with a totally new approach, new for him and
contemporary poetry. He is the master poet of his genre,
the only one continually and successfully to "ring true".'
Tribune

THE IRRELEVANT SONG

'A series of love poems, sensuous, erotic, intellectual
even ... quiet and restrained ... marked sensitivity and
eye for the unusual.'
The Guardian